Jason's
DRAGON

Published by BBC Books,
a division of BBC Enterprises Limited,
Woodlands, 80 Wood Lane, London W12 0TT

First published 1992

ISBN 0 563 36284 7

Set in Sabon Roman by Goodfellow & Egan, Cambridge
Printed and bound in Belgium by Proost N.V.
Colour separations by DOT Gradations Ltd., Chelmsford
Paper Case printed by Proost N.V.

Jason's
DRAGON

Written and illustrated by
ALAN BAKER

Edited by Linda Jennings

BBC BOOKS

"That garden's a jungle," said Dad.
Jason pricked up his ears. It was hot and sunny and just the right weather for exploring jungles. So, after packing his haversack, Jason set off on his trek.

The garden lay before him like a great ocean of grass. It seemed a long, long journey to the rose arch at the end of the lawn. The grass felt soft and springy under his feet.

Jason walked through the rose arch. He gazed at the rows of vegetables all around him.

"Dad should have been a farmer, not a gardener," he said.

For there were a multitude of magnificent marrows, tons of tiny tomatoes, billions of beans, and under some bumpy mounds were pounds and pounds of potatoes. Jason had never seen so many vegetables.

It was hot, very hot. Jason trudged through the rows of vegetables till he came to some rougher ground beyond. It was ages since he had been there.

"This is Dad's jungle," he said.

Jason blinked. The sun hurt his eyes.

He pushed his way through into some thick vegetation which shut out the fierce sun. It looked very wild and mysterious among the greenery. Brambles tore at his jeans and gnarled roots tried to trip him up. Then suddenly, the dense greenery opened up into a clearing, in the middle of which was a weed-covered pond.

Jason gazed dreamily into the murky green water. As he watched, a large crested newt swam slowly to the surface.

Jason looked at the newt, and the newt looked at Jason. There was something strange about it. Its smooth skin was turning into hundreds of shining scales, and two humps on its back fanned out into great dazzling wings.
It wasn't a newt. It was a dragon.
"Oh, you're *beautiful*," breathed Jason.
Then the dragon spoke,
"Jason the Explorer," he said in his strong dragon-voice, "If you really want to go exploring climb on to my back."

Even though he was a famous explorer, Jason was just a little afraid. But he took a deep breath and climbed on to the dragon's back.

"Hold tight!" said the dragon. It lowered its head and took several large bounds across the clearing, flapping its enormous wings. The dragon started to rise into the air. Jason looked down nervously as the ground rushed away from them and they rose above the treetops. Soon Jason's garden was just a tiny green patch below them.

"Where are we going?" shouted Jason.
His voice muffled against the wind.
   "I'm taking you to my home in the
mountains," said the dragon. "You can meet
all my friends."

Sure enough, way below them was a big purple
mountain, and as they drew nearer, Jason
could see the opening to a cave.
   "Brilliant!" he cried. "A real dragon's cave!"
The dragon flew nearer, flapping his wings
more slowly as they landed on the
mountainside.

Jason's eyes gradually became accustomed to the darkness inside the cave. It was like an enormous cathedral with pillars of rock rising from floor to ceiling. But, most amazing of all were the strange-looking monsters lining up to introduce themselves. There were Glumps and Squonks, Skarps and Gwarks, Trimmers and Skews, Hods and Purlers, Splats and Burrs. Jason felt quite confused. But though the monsters looked so strange they somehow seemed familiar. Where *could* he have met them before?

The dragon suddenly clapped his wings.

"Time for tea," he said, and all the monsters scurried away, reappearing with piles of brightly coloured cakes and fizzy drinks.

Jason bit into a cake cautiously. It was like a squidgy marshmallow, but much, much nicer.

In fact, it was the most delicious cake he had ever eaten.
  "That was lovely," he said when the feast was over,
  "But perhaps I should be getting home now."
  "You must visit our mountain first," said the
dragon. "Every explorer must climb a mountain."

Jason was pushed towards a doorway at the back of the cave. Beyond this was a steep flight of steps.

"Be careful!" said the dragon. "It's very slippery." It began to get colder. The steps wound upwards until Jason found himself on a snowy mountainside.

"We're nearly there now," said a Squonk from behind him.

Up and up and round and round they went.
It certainly was slippery and dangerous.
At last, huffing and puffing,
Jason reached the top.

Jason sat on the summit of the mountain to rest. It was wonderful, like sitting at the top of the world. Far below him he could see woods, rivers and patchwork fields. He could even see his own house with its garden like a speck of green and its pond like a flash of light.

"You must plant a flag," said the dragon. Jason fished in his haversack and brought out his red hanky. He broke a twig off a snow-covered tree and tied the hanky to it.

The monsters all jumped up and down with excitement.

"Three cheers for Jason the Explorer," they cried.

"Now I really *must* go home," said Jason. "Mum
will be worried." He began to make his way very
carefully down the slippery steps, and the dragon
and the monsters followed. Then everything started
to happen at once. Jason's feet slipped, and he fell on
his rucksack. The rucksack became a sort of sledge.

"Help!" cried Jason, and he began to slide, very fast,
down the mountainside. The dragon grabbed hold of
his haversack strap, and the monsters grabbed hold
of the dragon. They all followed Jason down the
mountain in a strange, rather terrifying procession.

They hurtled down the mountain, faster and faster. Jason swung the haversack from right to left to avoid the trees. Sometimes it seemed as if they would all land in a big painful heap.

Then, bump! Jason hit a large mound of earth, and tumbled over it, rolling down the slope on the other side. Splash! Down he went into a pond – his very own pond at the bottom of the jungle garden.

Jason scrambled from the water. He was soaked. Pond-weed clung to his T-shirt, and his boots were all muddy. He emptied his rucksack of pond-water. A large crested newt slid from its rock and disappeared into the depths.

Jason shook his head and blinked. That newt — had it *really* been a dragon? Or was it all a dream? Then he remembered. He looked in his haversack for his red hanky. It wasn't there.

So it wasn't a dream then. But where were all his new friends? Where were the Skarps, the Glumps, the Squonks and the Gwarks? Where were the Trimmers, the Skews, the Hods and the Purlers? Not forgetting the Splats and Burrs. Suddenly, Jason felt rather sad and lonely.

He wandered slowly back through the vegetable garden. Then he stared—very hard. There they were, all of them, hidden among the plants in his own garden, though you had to look carefully to find them.

No wonder they had all seemed so
familiar in the dragon's cave.

"Goodbye," said Jason. "Thanks for the
lovely tea."

"Come and visit us again," came a small
voice from among the big stripy marrows.

"I will," said Jason happily.
"Oh I will."

Squelch, squelch went Jason's wet boots as he
trudged home across the lawn. It was teatime.
Actually he didn't feel very hungry after eating
all those cakes. Mum would want to know why
he was all soaking wet and covered in pond-
weed. He would tell her all about the dragon
and the monsters.

But he doubted if she would believe him.